When a Dragon Comes to Stay

First published 2019 by Nosy Crow Ltd
The Crow's Nest, 14 Baden Place
Crosby Row, London SE1 1YW
www.nosycrow.com

Text © Caryl Hart 2019
Illustrations © Rosalind Beardshaw 2019

Magination Press
Books for Kids from the
American Psychological Association.

Adaptation copyright © 2021 by Magination Press, an imprint of the American
Psychological Association. All rights reserved. Except as permitted under the United States
Copyright Act of 1976, no part of this publication may be reproduced or distributed in any
form or by any means, or stored in a database or retrieval system, without the prior written
permission of the publisher.

Magination Press is a registered trademark of the American Psychological Association.
Order books at maginationpress.org, or call 1-800-374-2721.

Library of Congress Cataloging-in-Publication Data

Names: Hart, Caryl, author. | Beardshaw, Rosalind, illustrator.
Title: When a dragon comes to stay / Caryl Hart, Rosalind Beardshaw.
Description: [Washington, DC] : Magination Press, [2020] | Originally published: London:
Nosy Crow, 2019. | Summary: "Sometimes good manners can be a tiny bit tricky. Dragon
    demonstrates what it means to have good manners when she goes to visit"– Provided
    by publisher.
Identifiers: LCCN 2020019677 | ISBN 9781433834486 (hardcover)
Subjects: LCSH: Stories in rhyme. | CYAC: Manners and customs–Fiction. |
    Etiquette–Fiction. | Dragons–Fiction.
Classification: LCC PZ8.3.H251 Wf 2020 | DDC [E]–dc23
LC record available at https://lccn.loc.gov/2020019677

Printed in China

10 9 8 7 6 5 4 3 2 1

For Jess
C. H.

For the Fafa-Brooks,
with love, Rosi B x

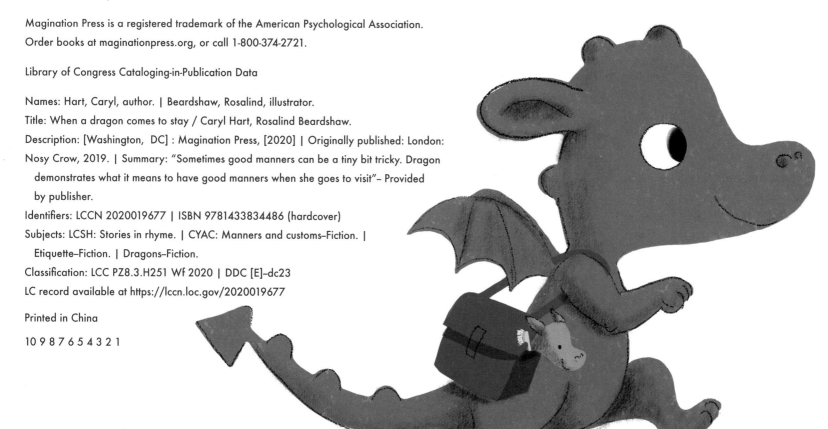

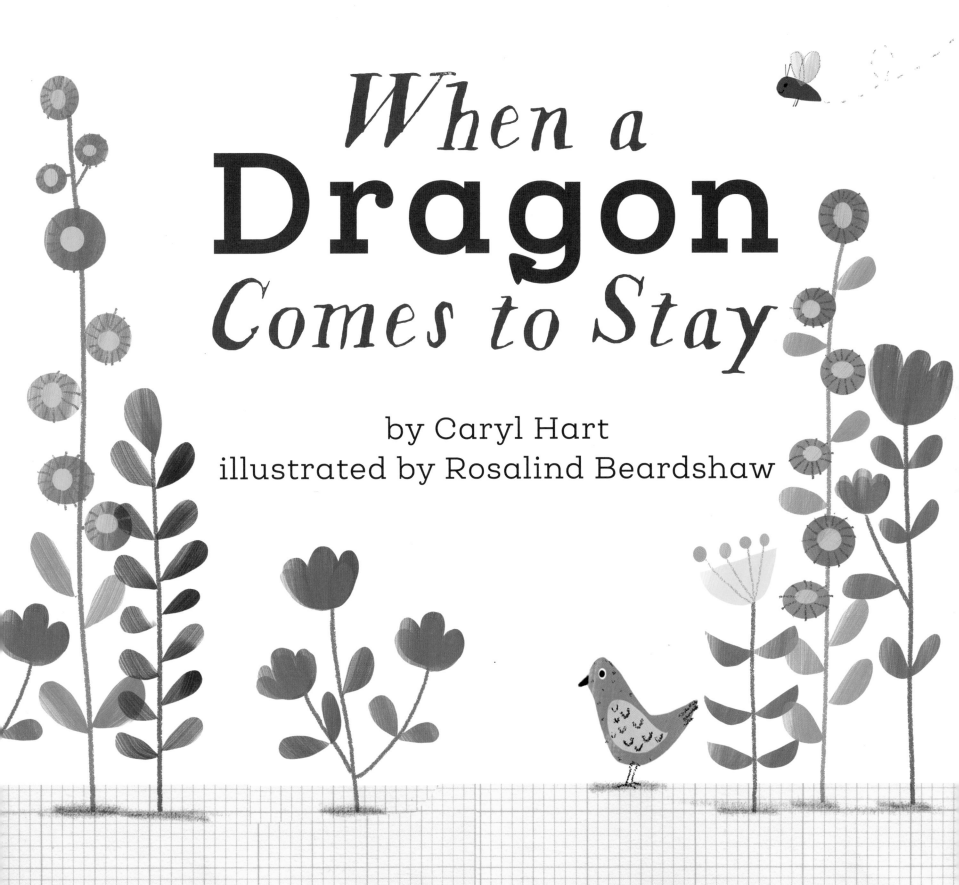

When a
Dragon
Comes to Stay

by Caryl Hart
illustrated by Rosalind Beardshaw

Magination Press • Washington, DC • American Psychological Association

When a **dragon** comes to stay . . .

. . . does she go ROAR!

and shout, "My way!"?

And does she snatch and keep the toys
away from other girls and boys?

Why, no! Dragons don't do that!

A dragon knows she must play fair
and wait her turn and **always** share.
She knows the rules of all the games
and **never** argues or complains
when she's the last to have a go.

That's just how dragons **are**, you know.

When playing games of hide-and-seek,
a dragon knows she must not **peek**.

She counts out loud to twenty-one,
then calls out, "Ready? Here I come!"
She never finds you right away.

That's just the way that dragons play.

At dinner, does a dragon slurp?
Or throw her food or moan or burp?

And does she spill food on the floor?
Or bang her spoon? Or bellow, "More!"?

Why, no! Dragons don't do that!

A dragon smiles and **sips** her tea
and eats her sandwich daintily.
She says the lettuce tastes **just right**
and never, ever gets a fright
at anything that's on her plate.

(Yes, dragons really **are** that great!)

And, when she's finished **all** her food,
a dragon is polite, not rude.
She takes her empty plate and cup . . .

and sometimes even washes up!
A dragon's **helpful** as can be.

It's just a dragon's **way**, you see.

Then, when the day is nearly done,
and we are tired from having fun,
do little dragons **wail** and moan?
Or **flap** their dragon wings and groan?

Why, no! Dragons don't do that!

She **skips** upstairs to take a bath.

Big bubbles make this dragon laugh!

She scrubs her dragon scales and wings.

All dragons **love** to do these things.

She puts some toothpaste on her brush,
then cleans her teeth. She **doesn't** rush.

She folds her wings up nice and **neat**
and pulls some bedsocks on her feet.
She doesn't make a **fuss**, or frown.

All dragons **like** to snuggle down.

Then, when it's time to go to bed,
does this small dragon shake her head?
Does this tired darling **cry** or pout?
Or **throw** her favorite toys about?

Why, no! Dragons don't do that!

But . . .

if she's overtired or sad,
that's when a dragon **might** turn bad.
Then you must wrap her in a hug,
and make her cozy, safe, and snug,
and sing a gentle dragon song.

A dragon **won't** stay sad for long.

So pull the cozy covers tight
to help her sleep all through the night.
She will not whine. She won't be roary.
All dragons **love** a bedtime story.
She'll listen very carefully.

How **lovely** can a dragon be?

ZZZZZZZ ZZ ZZ ZZ ZZ ZZ Z ZZ ZZ Z

And if her snores keep us awake,
and if they make the windows **shake**,
and if they **rumble** through the wall,

well ...

she is a dragon
after all!